The Dragon Who Lost His]

Tiny was a friendly dragon that lived on a mountain above Crystal Village.

Every Friday night the village folk would climb the mountain to spend time with Tiny.

One Friday evening something happened to Tiny, his fire turned into smoke rings.

Could the village folks help Tiny?

Did the plan work?

A fun filled adventure for parents to read to the children, or children to read themselves.

 For children's aged 4-10 by Kay Williams, illustrations by Danna Victoria.

Best wishes
Kay Williams

The Dragon Who Lost His Fire

Author Kay Williams

Illustrations by Danna Victoria

ISBN 978-0-9955317-7-2

Published by Cambria Books

Dedication

A big thank you to all my readers, who keep asking for more.

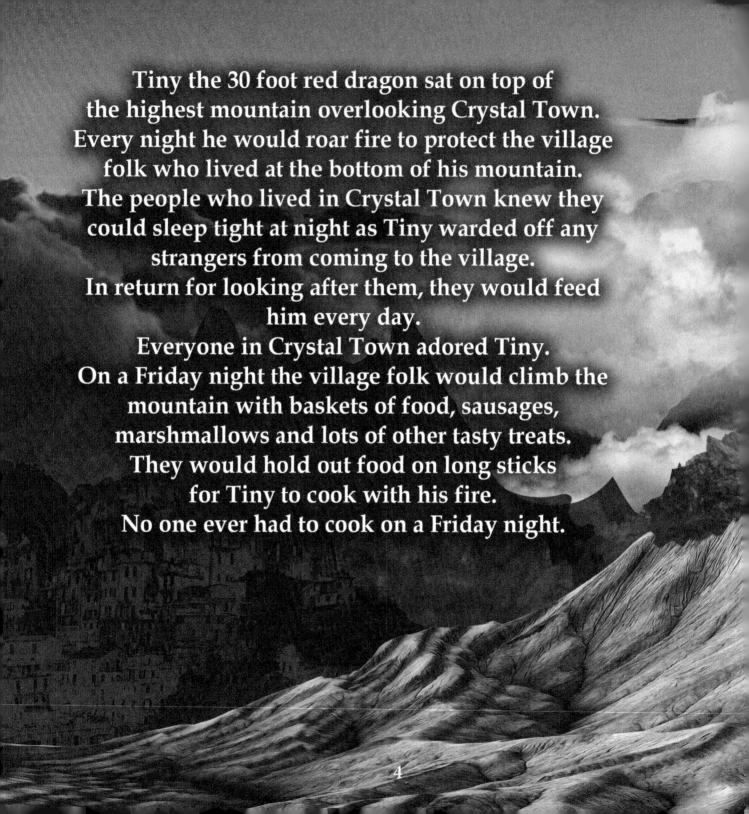

Tiny the 30 foot red dragon sat on top of
the highest mountain overlooking Crystal Town.
Every night he would roar fire to protect the village
folk who lived at the bottom of his mountain.
The people who lived in Crystal Town knew they
could sleep tight at night as Tiny warded off any
strangers from coming to the village.
In return for looking after them, they would feed
him every day.
Everyone in Crystal Town adored Tiny.
On a Friday night the village folk would climb the
mountain with baskets of food, sausages,
marshmallows and lots of other tasty treats.
They would hold out food on long sticks
for Tiny to cook with his fire.
No one ever had to cook on a Friday night.

The Mayor of Crystal Town was called Ethan. It was his job to hold the sausages on a stick while Tiny roared out his fire to cook them.

Next there was Peter. It was his job to the hold the marshmallows on a stick so Tiny's fire would cook them. Everyone in Crystal Town ate well on a Friday night.

A band would play as children danced and Tiny would breathe his fire to show his love for the people of Crystal Town.

At midnight, after goodbyes were said to Tiny, the village folk climbed back down the mountain and into their warm beds.

Once Tiny had watched to make sure everyone was home safe, he roared one more breath of fire and then he went to sleep.

It was such a relaxing place.

One Friday the village folk climbed the mountain
for Tiny to cook the food.
As always, Ethan held out the sausages.
Tiny breathed the fire gently over them and once
they were cooked perfectly, everyone ate.
Next, Peter stepped up with the marshmallows.
Tiny inhaled deeply and then blew out but this
time only rings of smoke came out.
There were no raging flames like normal.
He tried again but the very same thing happened.
Only smoke rings came out.
He wondered where his fire had gone.
Three more times he tried and only smoke
escaped from his mouth.
"What's wrong?" Ethan asked.
"Ethan, I do not know," answered Tiny.
"Stand back and let me try again."
Another two smoke rings escaped Tiny's mouth.
"You must be coming down with something Tiny.
Well, I think maybe it's our turn to look after you."
Peter said.

Doctor Green got out his medical bag and looked into Tiny's mouth. He had to use a big torch to look right inside because Tiny had such a very big mouth.

He'd never looked into a dragon's mouth before and he wasn't quite sure what he was looking for. He saw great big teeth, a large red tongue and two dangly bits at the back.

Ethan grabbed his legs while he leant to look further into Tiny's mouth. They didn't want him to fall in.

Once he'd had a good look, Doctor Green scratched his head. Nothing could explain why Tiny had lost his fire.

"You need rest. We will leave you in peace and Doctor Green will come back in the morning and see if you are any better," said Ethan.

The village folk worried that night.
They knew Tiny could not warn off any stranger
who might stumble across their little town.
When morning came Doctor Green climbed the
mountain to check on Tiny.
Again, he asked Tiny to breathe in and out.
Tiny coughed and spluttered and
out came two puffs of smoke.
"It's OK," said Doctor Green.
"I will find a cure for you."
Doctor Green went to the next village to
buy ingredients. He figured a potion might
make Tiny feel better.
He went to the herb shop and bought a basket
of herbs, a little packet of seeds and a small bottle
of liquid. He mixed the herbs and seeds together
with the liquid to make it easy for Tiny to swallow.
Then Doctor Green went straight back
to Crystal Town with his potion.

"Ethan I will need your help." he said.
Doctor Green and Ethan climbed the mountain with
the bowl of potion. It had turned into a nice soft
paste which would be easy for a big dragon
like Tiny to eat.
"Tiny I have made some medicine for you.
Would you let me put it in your mouth?"
asked Doctor Green.
"Well OK," replied Tiny, "but I do hope it doesn't
taste too bad."
"Ethan, I need you to hold my legs again.
I have to go to the very back of Tiny's mouth."
said Doctor Green.
"Not a problem Doctor," said Ethan.
Ethan was strong and it wouldn't be too difficult to
hold Doctor Green's legs, as long as
it didn't take too long.
"Tiny open wide and please try not to shut your
mouth while I am inside." said Doctor Green.
Doctor Green had to put his head and shoulders
into Tiny's mouth but Ethan held his legs tightly
so he wouldn't fall inside by accident.

"Hold me tighter Ethan! I have to crawl in a bit more!" shouted Doctor Green. His voice echoed up and out of Tiny's large mouth.
Ethan held onto Doctor Green's legs as firmly as he was able.
Doctor Green placed the paste at the back of Tiny's throat
"Tiny, as soon as I am free of your mouth you must swallow," said Doctor Green.
Ethan pulled on Doctor Green's legs to help him out. He was glad the Doctor had finished treating Tiny because the Doctor was heavier than he looked.
"Ok Tiny, now swallow," said the Doctor.
Tiny tried to swallow the medicine but couldn't. Instead he coughed and spluttered. Some puffs of smoke came out of his mouth and when he coughed again the medicine flew out and landed on Doctor Green's head! Ethan chuckled.
The Doctor did look funny standing there covered in Tiny's potion!

"I am sorry Dr Green," Tiny said.

"It is OK Tiny. We can try again," said the Doctor.

"Ethan, grab my legs! I am going in again!"

Again, Doctor Green tried but the same thing happened. Once more potion was put on his throat, Tiny coughed and spluttered and it all came back out again.

"I think we need Peter's help," said Doctor Green.

Ethan ran down the mountain to get Peter. Not long after both Peter and Ethan returned to help out.

"We came as quick as we could," said Peter.

"OK Doctor, what's the plan?" asked Ethan.

"You might not like this Ethan but you are going to have to come into Tiny's mouth with me," said Doctor Green.

"I will climb in first, Ethan you hold onto my legs like before and lower me into Tiny's mouth. Then Peter, you will have to hold Ethan's legs and lower us both in. Like a chain. You will be the anchor Peter.

That will mean I can get deeper into Tiny's throat to see what's wrong in there. Agreed?"

Peter and Ethan agreed. They cared for Tiny
so much, they were willing to do anything
it took to make him better.
"Tiny you might feel a little uncomfortable with
two of us in your mouth. Please keep your mouth
open at all times," said the Doctor.
"I will try Doctor Green," Tiny replied.
Doctor Green climbed in with Ethan
holding his legs.
"OK Peter, you hold Ethan's legs now and lower us
both down slowly. Don't either of you let go!"
When Doctor Green was at the very back of Tiny's
mouth he used the torch from his pocket and
looked around.
"Ethan steady me a minute. I think I can see
something!" he called back.
"Lower me just a little further."

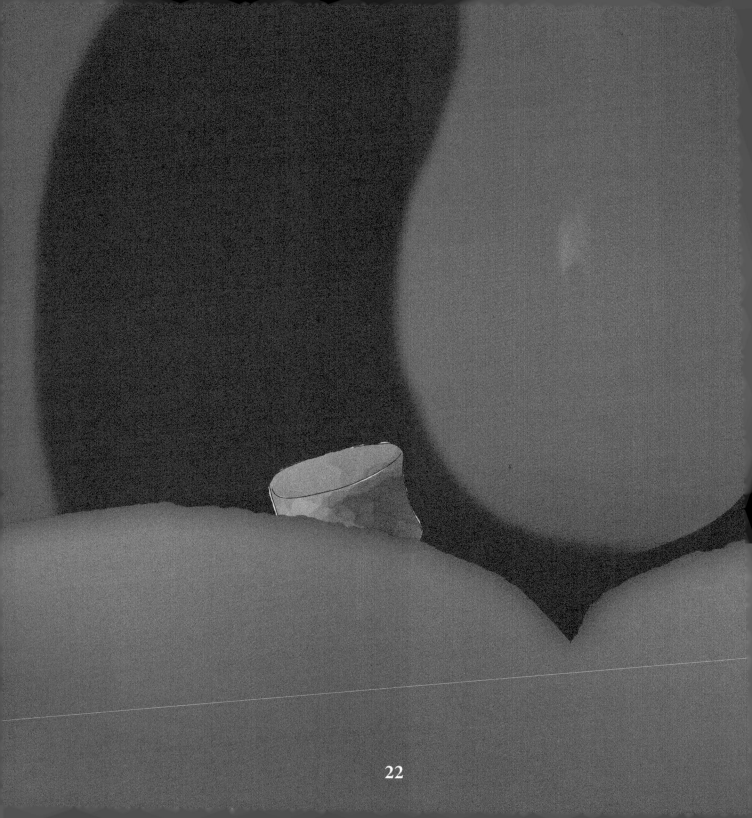

Ethan and Peter held tight as they lowered Doctor Green an extra few feet down. It allowed Doctor Green to be able to see right down into the huge dark tunnel that was Tiny's massive throat.

"Keep still Tiny!" shouted Dr Green.

"I think I see something." There was something pink and brown in the tunnel. "I have to get closer!" shouted Doctor Green. "Peter, can you lower us down any further?"

"I think so!" shouted Peter.

His voice echoed down into Tiny's throat.

Another foot or two and Doctor Green was able to reach the strange object. He wiggled it a bit and it made Tiny cough. Tiny's cough caused all three of them to fly out from his mouth and land with a thump onto the ground outside. Each of them were covered in thick gunk from Tiny's throat. Something else flew out and hit Doctor Green on his head. It was the pink and brown object he had been trying to wiggle loose.

"I'm so sorry everyone," said Tiny.
"You tickled me and I could not stop the cough."
The others got up and wiped off some of the gunk
from their clothes. It was a right mess!
Doctor Green went to examine the pink and brown
thing that followed him out of Tiny's mouth.
"Well I never!" he said.
"What?" asked Peter.
"I think I have found the problem,"
said Doctor Green.
He got a stick and held up the pink and brown thing.
It was a piece of marshmallow!
"Tiny you must have inhaled so hard when you were
cooking the marshmallows that a piece broke off
and jammed in the channel to your belly."
"How do you feel now Tiny?" asked Ethan.
"I feel a lot better thank you all," said Tiny.

"Well?" said Peter. "What are you waiting for?
Try out your fire to see if it works."
"Ok, here goes. Stand back," said Tiny.
He stood up to his full 30 foot in height.
He inhaled and then blew out as hard as he could.
A big orange jet of fire flew from his mouth.
Ethan, Peter and Doctor Green clapped happily.
"Well done Tiny!" said the Doctor.
The people of Crystal Town saw the fire and
climbed up the mountain to make sure Tiny
was feeling better.
Tiny felt so proud because he could protect
the village again.
He sat back comfortably on his large rock.
"I am still happy to cook for you all on a Friday
night." He smiled but added sternly,
"but no more marshmallows!"

Books in the series

Fido The Fish

Gizmo Escapes

Tiddles Caught In A trap

Jaws Gets Toothache

Snapper And The Hiccups

Bob And The Duck

Follow the series

Adventures In The Pond

Series Two of Adventures In The Pond coming in 2017

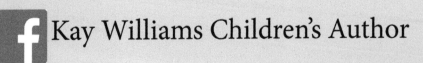 Kay Williams Children's Author

Lightning Source UK Ltd.
Milton Keynes UK
UKOW07f0836011216
288977UK00007B/33/P